This
**Power Rangers
Dino Thunder
Annual**
belongs to

▪▪▪▪▪▪▪▪▪▪▪▪▪▪▪▪▪▪

Contents

Written and edited by Brenda Apsley.
Designed by Peter Lawson.

EGMONT

We bring stories to life

Published in Great Britain 2005 by Egmont Books Limited,
239 Kensington High Street, London W8 6SA
Printed in Italy.
ISBN 1 4052 2103 8
10 9 8 7 6 5 4 3 2 1

Power Rangers Dino Thunder

When evil tyrant Mesogog sends his mutant warriors the Dino Zords to planet Earth, it's the job of high school teacher Doctor Tommy Oliver to try to stop him.

Revealing his secret past as Black Power Ranger, Tommy creates three new teen Power Rangers – Kira, Ethan and Conner – to take up the fight against evil.

But can the young singer, computer geek and soccer player make the grade as superheroes?

Day of the Dino
Part 1

On a wooded island, in a maze of dark underground tunnels, chaos reigned.

As a huge explosion created a shower of concrete fragments, smoke and dust, a hideous creature stepped from the shadows.

"FIND HIM!"

It was part human, part reptile – and its name was Mesogog.

The monster spoke to his servants, a pack of creatures called Tyranodrones. They were strong, fast, half human and half reptile and – like their master – totally evil.

"Find him," rasped Mesogog.

The man they were searching for was Doctor Thomas Oliver, better known as Tommy – and he knew enough about the Tyranodrones to know that escape was his only option.

RUN!

WHOOOSSHH!

When another explosion ripped through the tunnels and blasted him into the air, he picked himself up and ran to the exit. As he raced through the forest more explosions boomed and the ground shook.

KICK!

Tommy heard low snarls and growls from behind him and realised that the explosions were the least of his worries. Mesogog's Tyranodrones were tracking him – and they were gaining fast.

When the beasts finally caught up with Tommy, they surrounded him, then attacked. He fought them off, kicking out at them, but he was badly outnumbered.

Things were looking bad when there was another huge explosion right behind the Tyranodrones. It stunned some of Tommy's attackers, and he ran ...

SNARL!

Tommy ran as if his life depended on it – which it did – but he came to a screeching halt as the ground disappeared in front of him. He was standing on the edge of a sheer cliff with the ocean waves pounding the rocks a long, long way below.

"This is not good," he said as the Tyranodrones rushed towards him.

Tommy took one last look at them then took a deep breath – and leapt off the edge of the cliff!

He landed with a huge splash and disappeared under the pounding waves.

When the Tyranodrones peered over the cliff edge he was nowhere to be seen. Satisfied that he had met his fate, they turned back into the forest.

"THIS IS NOT GOOD!"

LEAP!

Minutes later the surface of the ocean broke and Tommy's head appeared. Choking and gasping, he took in big hungry gulps of air ...

As he looked back at the island there was another mighty explosion which erupted in a cloud of rock, soil and trees. When at last it died away the whole island collapsed and sank under the waves.

Tommy smiled a grim smile of satisfaction. He had escaped, and it was the Tyranodrones who had met their fate.

CHOKE! GASP!

KABOOM!

HE HAD ESCAPED!

"WHY?"

Some years later ...

Tommy was far, far away from the island.

It was his first day as science teacher at Reefside High School and the Principal, Mrs Randall, seemed suspicious of him. "Why would a doctor of palaeontology want to teach school kids?" she asked.

"I guess I'm looking for some peace and quiet," said Tommy.

Conner McKnight should have been one of the kids in Tommy's first class but he was out on the soccer pitch – until Mrs Randall found him. "Come with me!" she ordered.

When Mrs Randall found Kira Ford singing and playing her guitar she was in trouble too. "Please join us," she said.

"AAHH!"

"NEAT!"

As they crossed the lawn the water sprinklers came on and soaked Mrs Randall. Ethan James, the only student carrying an umbrella, had to be the one who had reprogrammed them.

"There's a week's detention for all three of you," said Mrs Randall. "Starting today."

After school Tommy was about to leave when Mrs Randall stopped him. "You're in charge of detention today," she said with a cruel smile.

"But I'm going to the dinosaur museum," said Tommy.

"That's fine," said Mrs Randall, pointing to Ethan, Kira and Conner. "You can take these monsters with you."

"So – er – you guys like museums?" asked Tommy.

"YOU GUYS LIKE MUSEUMS?"

Tommy was surprised to find that the museum was closed. "Take a look around while I find out what's happening," he said. "If you find any fossils I'll cancel detention, OK?"

Tommy found a notice: IN CASE OF EMERGENCY CONTACT ANTON MERCER INDUSTRIES.

"Anton Mercer," he said. "That's impossible."

When Tommy got back to the museum entrance a life-size replica Tyrannosaurus Rex came to life and attacked him! He ran for his car and took off, tyres smoking.

He raced to a low bridge and powered under it, but the T Rex slammed into it and fell to the ground. Its skin split open, revealing a shiny metal skeleton ...

SCREECH!

SLAM!

Out in the forest Ethan was uneasy. "Weird stuff happens out here," he said – as the ground gave way and he, Kira and Conner fell into a maze of underground passages.

When Conner got to his feet and touched a wall it opened up to reveal a hi-tech laboratory where a large gem-like rock shimmered and sizzled.

"Doctor Oliver wants fossils and that looks like one to me," said Conner and all three reached out and broke off a piece:

red for Conner,

yellow for Kira and

blue for Ethan.

YELLOW!

BLUE!

RED!

Rock in hand, Kira headed for the door. "Only a freak would live in a place like this," she said. "I don't want to be here when it gets home."

"We're right behind you," said Conner.

Ethan pointed: "There's the door."

Far, far away in his secret lair Mesogog sensed what had happened.

"The gems," he said. "They have moved. I – can – feel – them. Go. Bring them to me."

"I-CAN-FEEL-THEM!"

Seconds later a pack of snarling Tyranodrones surrounded the teens and started to move in.

"Run!" said Ethan.

Kira stumbled and her gem started to glow yellow. So did she!

"NOOOO!"

GLOW!

As a snarling Tyranodrone moved closer she screamed, "NOOOOO!" and the force of her voice hurled it into a tree!

Ethan's skin glowed blue! It had the texture of armour and when a Tyranodrone lashed out at him his skin was not marked or damaged.

When Conner's gem glowed red he found a strength and speed he didn't know he had.

All three fought the Tyranodrones until they disappeared as suddenly as they had arrived!

The teens were still taking it all in when Tommy arrived.

"You guys OK?" he asked.

GLOW!

"FORGET I WAS HERE!"

Later, back at school and alone again the teens agreed not to talk about what had happened.

"I can do better than that," said Kira, handing her rock to Conner. "Forget I was here, and I'll do the same."

But as she turned and walked away she heard familiar snarls and a horde of Tyranodrones grabbed her. They vanished – and they took Kira with them.

"Let's go to Doctor Oliver's house," Ethan said to Conner. "He knows about dinosaurs and these things are dinosaurs ... well, sort of."

There was no one at home, but the door was unlocked so Ethan and Conner went inside.

GRAB!

When Conner touched a dinosaur bone on the wall a trapdoor opened up beneath them – and they found themselves back in the same underground laboratory!

"Looking for something?" asked a voice behind them. It was Tommy!

"Doctor Oliver, we found these gem things in the forest and now Kira's been taken by some weird dinosaur things and ..." said Ethan.

Tommy didn't need to hear any more.

"The gems are Dino Gems and the dinosaurs are Tyranodrones," he said. "I worked on them with my partner, Anton Mercer – until he disappeared."

Conner and Ethan looked amazed. Tommy had a lot of explaining to do ...

"LOOKING FOR SOMETHING?"

YEAR BOOK

STAFF

Name:	Mrs Randall
Position:	Principal
Qualifications:	not known
Character:	stern, a believer in iron discipline

"My office – NOW!"

Name:	Doctor Thomas (Tommy) Oliver
Position:	science teacher
Qualifications:	Doctor of Palaeontology
Character:	kind and knowledgeable

"You don't like dinosaurs?"

STUDENTS

Name:	**Kira Ford**
Interests:	**singing** **songwriting** **playing guitar**
Ambition:	**to make it big in the** **music business**

"Whatever!"

Name:	**Conner McKnight**
Interests:	**soccer practice** **playing soccer** **girls**
Ambition:	**to be a star pro** **soccer player**

"Dude!"

Name:	**Ethan James**
Interests:	**gaming** **computer club** **surfing the web**
Ambition:	**to be the next computer** **billionaire**

"I'm groovin' to your tune."

Day of the Dino
Part 2

Far away in Mesogog's secret lair, Kira lay on a table groaning quietly.

Mesogog's green eyes glistened and flashed as he looked down at her. "Exxxxcellent," he rasped.

When Kira came to, Mesogog's face was the first thing she saw. "Where are the Dino Gems?" he hissed.

"You mean those rock things?" said Kira.

Mesogog hissed impatiently. "Yesssss."

"I gave mine to Conner and Ethan," said Kira. "You'll ..."

As she spoke Mesogog hissed in annoyance, then disappeared in a flash of light.

Suddenly a female robot appeared. "My master calls me Elsa," she said. "And this is Zeltrax."

"THOSE ROCK THINGS?"

"I'M ELSA."

"YESSSSS!"

Kira looked from the robot to a hideous monster and ran for the door. When she saw a glowing orb she reached out to it – and disappeared!

Outside his secret lab Tommy was telling Conner and Ethan more about the Tyranodrones. "I helped make them with Anton Mercer. They're really powerful but they weren't supposed to be used for evil. Our lab was destroyed and a monster called Mesogog stole all our research."

"And he's after these Dino Gem things we found?" said Conner.

Before Tommy could answer Ethan spoke. "Look, this isn't helping us find Kira," he said. "She's not just going to fall out of the sky in front of us and ..."

"I HELPED MAKE THEM."

Before he could say another word
Kira did just that!

"How did you do that?" asked Ethan.

"She came through an invisaportal,"
said Tommy. "It's a sort of gateway."

Before he could explain more there
were more arrivals: Zeltrax and a
swarm of Tyranodrones.

"WHAT?"

Zeltrax spoke to Tommy. "Come with me or you will suffer."

When Tommy refused the creatures attacked.

Kira screamed – loudly – at the Tyranodrone she was fighting
and was amazed to see it disappear.

Ethan was equally amazed when his shield–skin blocked
their blows.

"AAAEEEEE!"

BLOCK!

KICK!

Conner used his super-speed to attack a Tyranodrone from behind and kick it to the ground.

That left Tommy to face Zeltrax. "Tell your master Doctor Oliver's back," he said.

Zeltrax sneered. "I will tell him this battle is over – but the war has just begun." And with that he and the Tyranodrones disappeared.

Later, in his lair, it was Mesogog's turn to sneer. "Doctor Thomas Oliver. I should have known." He paused. "Zeltrax, is our aerial attack craft in position?"

"It is," answered Zeltrax.

"Good," said Mesogog. "When the Bio Zords have completed the first strike, launch the aerial assault. The citizens of Reefside won't know what's hit them."

"ATTACK!"

ROCK
SHAKE
RUMBLE

Next day at Reefside High, Tommy was taking a science class when the ground rumbled and the building rocked and shook. The sky outside turned from pale to deep blue to inky black.

Mrs Randall's voice came over the PA system. "Please remain calm," she told the students. "There is a state of emergency. You must go home. Now."

The students rushed out leaving Kira, Ethan, Conner and Doctor Oliver. He had a lot to explain in a very short time. "If Mesogog has sent the Bio Zords we've got to act fast. Come with me."

The teens exchanged a "what's going on?" look then followed him.

In the city a mighty Tricerazord rumbled along, wreaking havoc and leaving chaos and panic in its wake as cars were knocked into the air and people ran for their lives.

ROAR!

Far away Zeltrax watched and laughed. "The three Bio Zords are battling each other, Master!" he reported.

Tommy took the teens to his lab. "Bio Zords are like mechanical dinosaurs," he explained. "Fusion powered replicants that use actual dinosaur DNA for their neurofunctions."

"And you helped build them?" asked Ethan. He was seriously impressed.

Tommy nodded. "And YOU have to tame them. But you won't have to do it alone."

He opened a case and took out three objects. "Ever since I found the Dino Gems I've had these morphers ready in case I needed to harness their powers. They're Dino Morphers. You use them to become Power Rangers ..."

"Did you just say Power Rangers?" said Kira. "Us? But we can't be Power Rangers. Don't they have superhuman strength and stuff?"

"Yes, and you have those powers," said Tommy. "Look, I'll explain. Your gems are from an asteroid that crashed to Earth millions of years ago. It wiped out the dinosaurs. When I found the gems I realised how great their power was. I hid them so they wouldn't fall into the wrong hands."

"But us?" asked Conner.

"The Dino Gems are yours," said Tommy. "You didn't choose them. They chose you. They've bonded with your DNA to give you special powers."

"But this Mesogog and his creeps still want them?"

Tommy paused. "Yes, but the only way these powers can be taken from you is if you are destroyed."

"US?"

"THE GEMS CHOSE YOU."

28

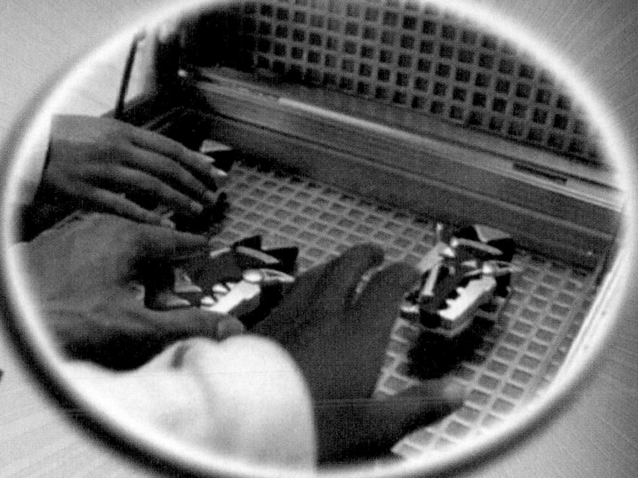

"DESTROYED?"

The teens shared a look.

"Look, the gems wouldn't have bonded with you if you couldn't handle the power," said Tommy, holding out the morphers. "Please?"

Ethan took the blue Dino Morpher. Conner took the red one. Kira took the yellow.

"Just say DINO THUNDER, POWER UP! and you'll be transformed into Power Rangers," said Tommy. "You've got to work together on this. You've got to believe in yourselves." He paused and looked from one to the other. "Because I believe in you."

"Really?" asked Conner.

"Really," said Tommy.

"REALLY."

Tommy and the teens drove into the city where the battle between the Zords was still going on. They were about to go into action when Zeltrax and a horde of Tyranodrones appeared.

"The only way you'll get to those Zords is by getting past me," said Zeltrax.

"That's the part we're looking forward to," said Conner. "Ready?"

Conner, Kira and Ethan spoke as one: "DINO THUNDER, POWER UP!"

"POWER UP!"

As all three morphed into Power Rangers for the first time they let out whoops and cries.

Tommy had to remind them that they had things to do. "Call up your weapons," he told them. "They're in your belts."

ZAP!

"I got a Tyranno Spear!" said Red Ranger. "Nice!"

"I can get to grips with these Ptera Grips," said Yellow Ranger.

Blue Ranger looked at his Tricera Shield. "Sweet!"

Zeltrax had seen enough: "ATTACK!"

The Tyranodrones launched a fierce attack.

"Combine your weapons!" Tommy ordered. "You have to tame the Zords. Concentrate. Hard. That way your morphers will communicate your thoughts to them."

"Calm down," said Blue Ranger. "I'm your friend. TRICERA ZORD!"

His morpher roared the message to the Triceratops Zord and it morphed into a friendly Zord.

"PTERA ZORD!" said Yellow Ranger. "We can be friends, right?"

Next, Tyranno Zord was tamed by Red Ranger.

"NICE!"

"GRIPS!"

"SWEET!"

ATTACK!

The Power Rangers were absorbed into their own Zords.

"Now bring them together," said Tommy. "You can do it."

"Combine powers!" cried the Power Rangers, and three Zords became mighty Thundersaurus Megazord.

Zeltrax's ship closed in, firing lasers. Tentacles shot from it, entangling the Megazord, and the Rangers were hit by a powerful sting beam.

Thundersaurus Megazord swung though the air on one of the tentacles until it was above the heart of Zeltrax's ship.

"Dino Drill, engage!" ordered Blue Ranger.

As the Rangers looked on the ship exploded.

BOOM!

KAPOW!

STING!

"HISSS!"

The event did not go unnoticed by Mesogog. "Ssssso, Oliver has taught them to become Rangers, has he?" he hissed.

The battle won, Tommy took Ethan, Conner and Kira to his lab where the three morphers changed into bracelets, each with a coloured gem. The teens took one each.

"Keep these with you," said Tommy. "They'll access your morphers and you can use them to communicate with me – and with each other."

He looked from Ethan to Kira to Conner. "Look, I know this is a lot to take in," he said. "Your lives have changed in ways you couldn't have imagined. But if you work as a team no one can defeat you." He paused. "No one."

Power Ranger Profile

Red Ranger

NAME: Conner McKnight

AGE: 17 years

OCCUPATION:	high school student
SPECIAL INTEREST:	soccer
RANGER DESIGNATION:	Red Ranger
ZORD:	Tyrannosaurus
WEAPON:	Tyranno Spear
RANGER MODES:	Normal mode
	Dino mode
	Triassic mode
SPECIAL ABILITIES:	super-strength
	lightning-fast speed

CHARACTER: Conner may be a student but his mind is rarely on his high school studies. He's much more concerned with his great love, soccer — and girls.

Conner's physical strength and skills make him a power to be reckoned with on the soccer pitch and he has high hopes of becoming a pro player one day. He's the star of the Reefside High soccer team, the best and most talented player by far — but he doesn't always remember the importance of playing as part of a team.

Since the Dino Gem chose him to become Red Ranger, Conner has also put his strength and speed to good use on the battlefield. Now he's part of an even more important team and must learn that he has to work with Blue and Yellow Rangers when it comes to protecting the Earth.

"Dino Thunder, Power Up!"

Power Ranger Profile

 **Blue Ranger**

NAME: Ethan James

AGE: 17 years

OCCUPATION: high school student

SPECIAL INTEREST: playing computer games

RANGER DESIGNATION: Blue Ranger

ZORD: Triceratops

WEAPON: Tricera Shield

RANGER MODES: Normal mode

Dino mode

SPECIAL ABILITY: generates armour-like skin which is able to withstand injury

CHARACTER: There's not a lot Ethan doesn't know about computers. Some people might call him a computer geek, but there's much more to him than that.

Ethan might have used his computer know-how to make mischief in the past, but now the Dino Gem has chosen him to become Blue Ranger, he uses his wealth of skills and knowledge to help protect planet Earth.

Ethan's favourite place to hang out is Hayley's Cyberspace, a hip café where he can surf the net and play his favourite computer games. Now that he's a Power Ranger Ethan has to learn that he isn't going to save the world sitting in front of a computer screen — there's a real world with real dangers out there, and he has to be in it.

"Dino Thunder, power up!"

Power Ranger Profile

Yellow Ranger

NAME: Kira Ford

AGE: 17 years

OCCUPATION:	high school student
SPECIAL INTEREST:	singing, songwriting and playing guitar
RANGER DESIGNATION:	Yellow Ranger
ZORD:	Pteranodon
WEAPON:	Ptera Grips
RANGER MODES:	Normal mode
	Dino mode
SPECIAL ABILITY:	generates power sonic screams

CHARACTER: Kira lives for music. She spends all her free time — and even short breaks at school — singing and playing her guitar for whoever will listen. When she isn't singing and playing, she's songwriting.

Her greatest hope is that she and her band, The Cause, will make it big one day. It's not the fame she craves, just the chance to communicate with people through her music.

Kira has a fiery personality and now that she's been chosen by the Dino Gem to become Yellow Ranger, she's using the drive that makes her determined to be a star one day to help her save the Earth.

"Dino Thunder, power up!"

Power Ranger Assessment:
Skills Test 1

Power Rangers need amazing strengths and skills. Do you have what it takes to be a Ranger?

Test your abilities by completing the series of ten Ranger skills tests in this annual. Keep a note of your answers, then turn to page 68 to check them – and find out your personal Power Ranger skills rating.

1 It's all in the detail

Power Rangers need to take in information – fast. Can you answer these questions based on Day of the Dino? Careful – some are tricky!

1 Doctor Thomas Oliver is better known as Timmy. True or false?

2 Is the school where Doctor Oliver teaches called
a) Stateside   b) Reefside or   c) Seaside?

3 What subject does Doctor Oliver teach?

4 What is the name of the school Principal?

5 Which student programmed the sprinkler system so that the Principal got soaked?

6 Is Kira's second name
a) Ford   b) Forge or   c) Forest?

7 Which replica dinosaur came to life at the museum?

8 What kind of evil creatures attacked the teens in the forest?

9 When the dinosaur chasing Doctor Oliver crashed into the bridge what kind of skeleton was revealed under its skin?

10 Which Power Ranger uses the Ptera Grips?

Points SCORE 1 point for each correct answer.

Target 10 points

Time limit 5 minutes

40

Coded message

Sometimes the Power Rangers need to communicate in code. Can you decipher this message? Fill in each square using its letter–number code. The first is done as an example.

b2 d4 b4 c6 c8 b6 e14 b14 c20 c22 i13 l9 b3 f7 c4 f16

b7 e21 b18 d18 e6 f22 d22 e2 e12 b17 h14 f18 b16 h13 d16

k11 i9 c2 b8 b22 e20 b10 c10 e8 j15 l10 d3 d20 f20 d8 i15

f13 f17 c16 d17 l11 f6 d21 b20 h11 b21 c14 e16 e10 k13 j11 d2

d6 j14 d10 d12 d14 h15 i11 j9 f2 f8 j13 f11 f12 h9 k9 l13

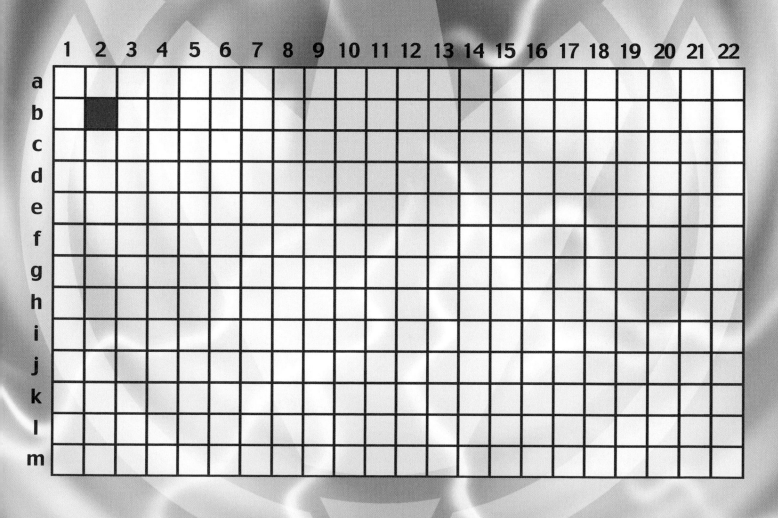

Points SCORE 10 points
for revealing the message.

Target
10 points

Time limit
10 minutes

The next tests are on page 46.
Remember to turn to page 68 to check your answers.

ENEMY ALERT!

NAME: MESOGOG

ALIAS: DOCTOR ANTON MERCER

AGE: UNKNOWN

AIM: TO RETURN THE EARTH TO ITS PREHISTORIC ORIGINS

SPECIAL ABILITIES: PSIONIC POWERS
TELEKINESIS
TELEPATHY

"Bring - me - the - Dino Gemsssss!"

ENEMY ALERT!

Some years ago, Doctor Anton Mercer was a successful and respected scientist. Working with Doctor Thomas Oliver he developed the Tyranodrones and Bio Zords.

But when Mercer's laboratory was destroyed the precious research was lost to the world. Or was it? For not only did Anton Mercer disappear – he took his secrets with him. Whilst taking part in a doomed experiment Mercer was taken over by an evil entity which used not only his body, but his mind as well. That entity is ... Mesogog!

The two personalities now sharing the same hideous form are at war with each other. They fight an ongoing battle to control the body they share. But Mesogog is winning, and monitors events on Earth from the secret lair where he watches – and waits ...

His aim is to return the planet Earth to its prehistoric roots. He needs a huge power source to do this: the Dino Gems. It is their great power that he craves. The fact that the power of the Dino Gems can only be obtained if the Power Rangers are destroyed does not concern him: they are expendable.

"The Power Rangersss? Desssstroy them!"

File Under: ENEMY

NAME:	**ELSA**
ALIAS:	MRS RANDALL, PRINCIPAL OF REEFSIDE HIGH SCHOOL
AGE:	UNKNOWN
SPECIAL ABILITIES:	ANDROID SUPER-STRENGTH DESTRUCTIVE ENERGY PROJECTION
SPECIAL INTEREST:	SERVING HER MASTER, MESOGOG
DISLIKES:	RED RANGER

Elsa is a cyborg servant, a tough and ruthless fe-bot. Her only role and desire is to obey her master, Mesogog. She has a particular dislike of Red Ranger and will try anything to defeat him.

NAME:	**ZELTRAX**
ALIAS:	SMITTY
AGE:	UNKNOWN
SPECIAL ABILITIES:	DESTRUCTIVE ENERGY PROJECTION ENDURANCE
SPECIAL INTEREST:	SERVING HIS MASTER, MESOGOG
DISLIKES:	DOCTOR OLIVER

Zeltrax is one of Mesogog's cyborg servants. He knows one thing and one thing only: to obey his master. As Smitty he once competed with Doctor Oliver for a job at Anton Mercer's laboratory. When the job went to Tommy, Smitty decided that he would work on alone. His dangerous experiments led to disaster and when Mesogog found his battered body and rebuilt it using cybernetic technology, Smitty – transformed into Zeltrax – was his for ever.

"GRUNT!"

NAME:	**TYRANODRONES**
NUMBER:	**TOO MANY TO COUNT**
SPECIAL ABILITIES:	**ENDURANCE**
	SUPER STRENGTH
SPECIAL INTEREST:	**SERVING MESOGOG**

"SNARL!"

"SNARL!"

"GRUNT!"

The Tyranodrones were genetically engineered using dinosaur DNA by Tommy and Anton Mercer. They were created as a force for good but now they act only for evil as the faceless minions and servants of Mesogog.

The Tyranodrones are ruthless, determined and very, very powerful. They do not speak but communicate in grunts and snarls. They do only as they are commanded by their master.

Match up

3

Can you draw lines to join Kira, Ethan and Conner to their symbols and special weapons?

46

Points SCORE 5 points if you made the right links.

Target 5 points

Time limit 2 minutes

Observation test A

Power Rangers need excellent visual skills. Are you as observant as they have to be? These pictures look the same, but there are five things that are missing in picture 2. Can you identify all five?

Points SCORE 1 point each time you spot a part missing.

Target 5 points

Time limit 3 minutes

Observation test B

Can you spot the imposters from the real thing? Which is the real Zeltrax? (Tip: look back at page 44.)

1

2

3

4

5

6

Points SCORE 5 points for a correct answer.

Target 5 points

Time limit 2 minutes

The next tests are on page 54.
Remember to turn to page 68 to check your answers.

The Fight Goes On ...

Tommy introduced Kira, Ethan and Conner to another new member of the Power Rangers team. The teens already knew Hayley as the owner of a Cyberspace cafe where they had started to hang out. But they found out that she did a lot more than make coffee. She was an old friend of Tommy's, a techno legend and programming genius who got tired of big business and opened the cafe instead. Now she's the Power Rangers' technical wizard.

The teens were stunned when Tommy told them he used to be a Ranger – Black Ranger. He also told them more about his work. When the island exploded, some of the things he'd been working on were scattered – but they were not lost forever.

He showed them some large eggs. "We're going to hatch them," he explained. "Then you're going to ride them! They're robotic raptors – I call them Raptor Riders."

When **Trent Fernandez** arrived in Reefside he started working at Hayley's Cyberspace as a waiter, but soon very weird stuff started happening to him. He saw visions of himself changing into a powerful superhero figure dressed in white. What he was seeing was himself morphing into White Dino Ranger – he just didn't know it yet! Something else he didn't know was that the difference between White Ranger and the other Power Rangers was that he was under Mesogog's control and was used as a force not for good – but for EVIL!

There was one more thing Trent didn't know. His dad was **Anton Mercer,** Tommy's old partner and the guy whose body had been taken over by Mesogog. When Trent went into an invisaportal in his father's office one day, he asked his dad about the weird stuff that was happening. But Mercer wouldn't explain right then. "In time," he told Trent. "For now, all I can tell you is that what's going on is for the safe future of mankind."

Trent was left to wonder just what that meant ...

Power Ranger Profile

Black Ranger

NAME: Doctor Thomas Oliver

AGE: unknown

OCCUPATION: high school science teacher

SPECIAL INTEREST: palaeontology

RANGER DESIGNATION: Black Ranger

ZORD: Brachiosaurus

WEAPON: Brachio Staff

RANGER MODES: Normal mode

Dino mode

SPECIAL ABILITY: can make himself invisible

CHARACTER: What seems like a lifetime ago, top palaeontologist Doctor Tommy Oliver did some amazing experiments with his colleague Doctor Anton Mercer in which they successfully combined dinosaur DNA with modern technology. But when their lab was destroyed they lost all their work and Mercer disappeared.

When Tommy obtained the black Dino Gem from evil Mesogog, it chose him to become Black Ranger.

Now Tommy works as a science teacher at Reefside High School, but he still has a secret lab at his home where he devises new weapons for the Power Rangers with the help of his friend Hayley.

"Dino Thunder, power up!"

Power Ranger Profile

White Ranger

NAME: Trent Fernandez

AGE: 17 years

OCCUPATION: high school student
part-time waiter

SPECIAL INTEREST: drawing and painting

RANGER DESIGNATION: White Ranger

WEAPON: Drago Sword

RANGER MODES: Normal mode
Dino mode

SPECIAL ABILITIES: can blend into his surroundings
and remain unseen
super fast
able to draw arrows with his
Drago Sword

CHARACTER:

Trent seems quiet and shy, but that doesn't mean he's not super-observant, a trait that's obvious when you see the detail in his drawings.

He's the secret son of Doctor Oliver's one-time colleague, Doctor Anton Mercer — once the evil White Ranger — who has come to live in Reefside City.

Trent doesn't get on with his father, who thinks his artwork is a waste of time, and he prefers working as a waiter at Hayley's Cyberspace to spending time at home.

WARNING

THERE'S AN EVIL COPY OF WHITE RANGER SOMEWHERE OUT THERE, AND HE CAN DO WHATEVER TRENT CAN DO ...

Power Ranger Assessment: Skills Test 3

Ready for more Power Ranger tests? Remember to keep a note of your answers.

Identities

6 Can you find these names and words in the word square? Tick each one you find; there are 15.

ANTON BLACK BLUE CONNER ELSA ETHAN HAYLEY KIRA MESOGOG RED TOMMY TRENT WHITE YELLOW ZELTRAX

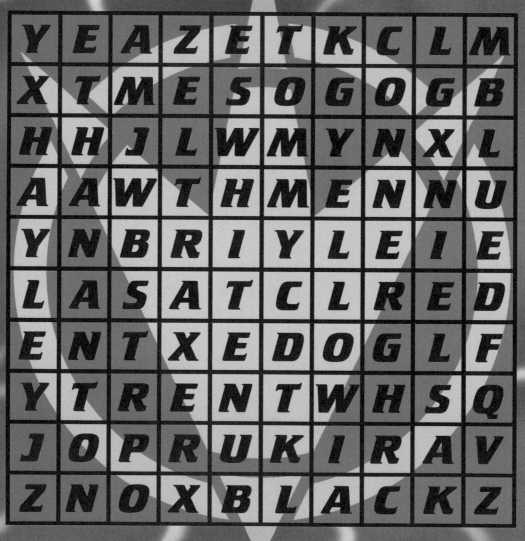

Y	E	A	Z	E	T	K	C	L	M
X	T	M	E	S	O	G	O	G	B
H	H	J	L	W	M	Y	N	X	L
A	A	W	T	H	M	E	N	N	U
Y	N	B	R	I	Y	L	E	I	E
L	A	S	A	T	C	L	R	E	D
E	N	T	X	E	D	O	G	L	F
Y	T	R	E	N	T	W	H	S	Q
J	O	P	R	U	K	I	R	A	V
Z	N	O	X	B	L	A	C	K	Z

Points SCORE 1 point for each name you find. Add a bonus of 5 points if you find all 15 words, making 20 points in all.

Target 20 points **Time limit** 10 minutes

Copy

7

This is White Ranger. But there's an evil copy of him, too. Can you identify it?

1

2

3

4

5

6

Points SCORE 5 points if you identify the copy correctly.

Target
5 points

Time limit
3 minutes

Turn to page 66 for the final test.
Remember to turn to page 68 to check your answers.

White Thunder
Part 1

It was the middle of the night and Hayley's Cyberspace cafe was in darkness. But it wasn't silent ...

When Hayley went to investigate the noise that had woken her she found ... Trent. He was sitting on the floor with a sketch pad and pencil.

"I have a question," said Hayley.

"What am I doing here when I should be home in bed?" asked Trent.

"That would be the one," said Hayley.

"I came to draw in peace," said Trent. "My dad's not keen on my art, thinks it's a waste of time. Says it won't get me anywhere. I tend not to draw when he's around."

SLURP

In his lair Mesogog was making plans. "Doctor Oliver beware. We are nearly ready to equalise our forces and go head to head with the Dino Rangers," he told Zeltrax.

Just then a large spider appeared in front of Mesogog. He flicked out his long tongue, curled the spider into his mouth – and chewed.

CHEW

Elsa was playing her part in Mesogog's plan. At that moment she was in a strange forest, trying to locate a carbon infusion with the infrared vision built into her sunglasses. "The energy should be almost ready now," she said. She opened up a laptop computer, hit a button, and an "eye" on its cover fired strange waves from it.

"FIRE!"

The waves ceased and Elsa smiled as she saw the results: a huge Tyrannosaurus Rex and two Pterodactyls.

Elsa put on a pair of headphones and typed instructions on the keyboard. She said, "Fire!" and the waves created an explosion that rocked the forest. It forced Elsa to duck for cover as sound waves swept through the trees. When she saw the result of the explosion Elsa smiled. Her master, Mesogog, would be very pleased.

BEEP!

"WHO'S THAT!"

Far away, a beep in Tommy's lab alerted him to events. "Who's that?" he said as he looked at a monitor and saw Elsa and the site where she had created the explosion. "A petrified forest?" he said. Tommy was puzzled. **"What's going on out there?"**

Raptor Thunder

Use the small picture of Yellow Ranger and Raptor Rider to help you colour in the larger one.

WARRIORS AGAINST EVIL

Use the small picture of Red Ranger and Raptor Rider to help you colour in the larger one.

RAGING RAPTORS

White Thunder
Part 2

Tommy and the teens were wondering where the missing White Dino Gem might be.

"If we can't find the gem is that good news – or bad?" asked Conner.

"That depends on who has the gem," Tommy answered.

What they didn't yet know was that the White Dino Gem was in Mesogog's lair – and so was Trent Fernandez!

The morpher wrapped itself around his wrist and he saw visions of himself as White Ranger.

Soon the visions were gone and he was in action for real, but he was fighting for Mesogog and evil AGAINST the Power Rangers. "I'm here for one thing," he told them. "To defeat you."

White Ranger fired energy from his hand at a Dino Egg he was holding.

"The energy transfer will activate Dino Zord," he said to it. "Soon you will be ready. And then there will be only one colour left in the rainbow – white."

ENERGY!

Later Ethan and Kira were in Hayley's Cyberspace. "Have you seen Trent?" asked Hayley. "He's a good waiter, but he's ..."

Trent finished the sentence for her as he walked in through the door. "... late. Yeah, sorry about that."

Trent got to work and was on his way to a table with a tray of drinks when he stopped, stumbled and fell forward. The tray hit the floor and mugs and glasses smashed.

"Are you OK?" asked Hayley. "You look kinda strange."

"Well, things have been a little – weird lately," said Trent. "Sorry, Hayley, I ... er ... just lost it for a second there. I'll be OK."

What Trent couldn't tell Hayley, or anyone else, was that it was seeing weird visions of himself as White Ranger that had made him stumble and fall.

"Look, you're exhausted, take some time off," said Hayley. "Go."

Trent hesitated but he knew when not to argue with Hayley and made for the door.

"Look, will you call me later to let me know you're OK?" said Hayley. **But Trent was gone ...**

SMASH!

"ARE YOU OK?"

Raptor Thunder

Use the small picture of Blue Ranger and Raptor Rider to help you colour in the larger one.

RAPTOR POWER

Use the small picture of
Black Ranger and Raptor
Rider to help you colour
in the larger one.

RAPTOR RAGE

White Thunder
Part 3

In the city, battle commenced between Drago Zord and Thundersaurus Megazord.

White Dino Ranger sat on Drago Zord's head. "Show these fools what you can do," he said, leaping to the ground.

Drago Zord flapped its wings, creating huge gusts of wind that lifted clouds of debris into the air. Even Thundersaurus Megazord struggled to keep its balance.

"NO!" yelled Tommy.

More flaps and gusts lifted cars into the air like toys. Sparks and debris flew around and Thundersaurus Megazord was forced to step back.

Drago Zord flapped its wings and the city filled with clouds of dust and debris. It took off into the sky then swooped down again, hitting Thundersaurus Megazord each time.

"We need Stega Zord!" said Tommy.

"I hoped you'd say that," said White Ranger. He waved his Drago Sword and Stega Zord glowed gold. "You are under my command! Dino Stega Zord formation!" he commanded.

Drago Zord gripped Stega Zord and flew up high above the city. Then Drago Zord split into pieces and reformed as the new Megazord formation.

"He's got his own Megazord!" said Tommy.

"Not bad for a new guy, huh?" said White Ranger.

Dino Stega Zord slashed Thundersaurus with its mighty sword – until Tricera Zord's horns caught the blade.

Ethan called, "Tricera Fist!" and it broke Dino Stega Zord's hold.

When Conner called up the Tyranno Drill Thundersaurus Megazord attacked with it.

"Dino Stega Zord Stinger – intercept!" said White Ranger and a ball of energy shot the stinger missile at Thundersaurus Megazord. It hit home and the Rangers' cockpit malfunctioned big time.

The Dino Zords split apart and the Rangers fell to the ground. Their Zords powered down – then slept.

White Ranger held his glowing Drago Sword. "Now I'll take the rest of the Zords."

"I don't think so," said Tommy, successfully reversing the transformation of the Dino Stega Zord.

"You'll pay for that," said White Ranger as Drago Zord flew off.

"Good save, Doctor Oliver!" said Ethan.

Tommy smiled. "Somehow I don't think it'll be the last."

For the Power Rangers, the fight against evil goes on ...

The battle is over, but the war has just begun ...

Power Ranger Assessment:
Skills Test 4

This is the final Power Rangers skills assessment. It's your last chance to boost your score, so POWER UP — there are 40 points to be won!

White thunder

Can you answer these questions on the White Thunder story?

1 Is Hayley's café called
a) Cyberspace b) Cybercafé or c) Cyberborg?

2 Who made the noise that woke Hayley?

3 What kind of creepy-crawly did Mesogog eat?

4 What job does Trent have at Hayley's?

5 What is the name of White Ranger's special weapon? Is it
a) Drago Shield b) Drago Sword or c) Drago Staff?

6 Whose horns caught the blade of Dino Stega Zord's sword?

7 What pastime does Trent enjoy? Is it
a) skateboarding b) soccer or c) drawing?

8 What flapped its mighty wings filling Reefside City with clouds of dust and debris?

9 Who wore infrared vision sunglasses?

10 Who called up the Tyranno Drill?

Points SCORE 1 point for each correct answer.

Target 10 points

Time limit 5 minutes

Decode needed

Can you decode this message?
Write a letter for each number.

1	2	3	4	5	6	7	8	9	10	11	12	13	14	15	16	17	18	19	20	21	22	23	24	25	26
w	x	y	z	a	b	c	d	e	f	g	h	i	j	k	l	m	n	o	p	q	r	s	t	u	v

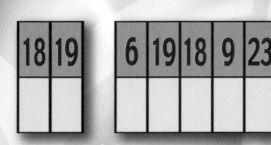

18	19

6	19	18	9	23

5	6	19	25	24

13	24

Points
SCORE 1 point for each correct letter. Add a 6–point bonus if you spell out the full message.

Target
20 points

Time limit
5 minutes

Thunder

Careful! Which two Thunder icons are identical?

1 **2** **3**

4 **5** **6**

Points
SCORE 10 points if you identify the pair.

Target
10 points

Time limit
3 minutes

Now check your score on page 68.

Power Ranger Assessment Tests: the Result

Check your answers to the Power Ranger assessment tests 1, 2, 3 and 4.

1   It's all in the detail
1. false, it's Tommy; 2. b, Reefside; 3. science; 4. Mrs Randall; 5. Ethan James;
6. a, Ford; 7. Tyrannosaurus Rex; 8. Tyranodrones; 9. metal; 10. Yellow Ranger.

2   Coded message
POWER UP

3   Match up
Conner, red symbol and Tyranno Spear; Ethan, blue symbol and
Tricera Shield; Kira, yellow symbol and Ptera Grips.

4   Observation test A
The following are missing:
1. part of weapon; 2. toe;
3. part of helmet; 4. arm badge;
5. part of fist.

5   Observation test B
Number 2 is Zeltrax.

6   Identities

```
Y E A Z E T K C L M
X T M E S O G O G B
H H J L W M Y N X L
A A W T H M E N N U
Y N B R I Y L E I E
L A S A T C L R E D
E N T X E D O G L F
Y T R E N T W H S Q
J O P R U K I R A V
Z N O X B L A C K Z
```

7   Copy
Number 4 is the copy.

8   White thunder
1. a, Cyberspace; 2. Trent; 3. a spider; 4. waiter; 5. b, Drago Sword; 6. Tricera Zord;
7. c, drawing; 8. Drago Zord; 9. Elsa; 10. Conner (Red Ranger).

9   Decode needed
No bones about it

10   Thunder
Numbers 1 and 5 are identical.

Write your scores in the chart then add up your points. There are 100 to be won!

test 1	target	10	your score	
test 2	target	10	your score	
test 3	target	5	your score	
test 4	target	5	your score	
test 5	target	5	your score	
test 6	target	20	your score	
test 7	target	5	your score	
test 8	target	10	your score	
test 9	target	20	your score	
test 10	target	10	your score	
POINTS TOTAL	100		YOUR TOTAL SCORE	

How did you score?

0-30	as Conner would say, that's the pits, man!
30-50	so-so, but could be SO much better
50-70	that's a bit more like it – you're trying
70-90	wow! now you're really motoring
over 90	what a result! – when can you join?
100	awesome – you sure you're not already a Power Ranger?

DIPLOMA

**Well done, you've earned your place alongside the Power Rangers so fill in your name and age on the diploma.
Now YOU can join the battle against evil and help save planet Earth!**

Name _____

Age _____

Add a photograph or drawing of yourself and choose your personal Power Ranger name, skill and weapon.

**Power Ranger
Name** _____

Skill _____

Weapon _____